Happy Ever After

A Pandemic Tale

by Dr Marlene MD
DrMarleneMD@DrMarleneMD.com

illustrated by Andrew M
andym.illustration@gmail.com

For permission requests, write to the author, addressed "Attention:Permissions" at DrMarlene@DrMarleneMD.com

Website: www.DrMarleneMD.com

Ordering information on website www.DrMarleneMD.com

Available for purchase at online book retailers, ebook retailers, independent bookstores, chain stores, and online stores

For details, contact DrMarlene@DrMarleneMD.com

Print ISBN: 9781088029282

Printed in the United States of American

First Edition

Dedicated with love to:
The happiness of my
grandchildren,
Alia Eve and Ashton Tucker.
Thanks for being you!

Timmy Turtle has a friend, Speedy Seagull.
Speedy says, "I cannot fly super-fast.
My zoom superpower is not working.
I think a virus is causing this problem."

Timmy asks, "Is the virus in town?"
Speedy says, "I will fly over the town."

A virus can cause a disease.
Sometimes, it is more than a sneeze.

The virus is everywhere. It is a pandemic.
A pandemic is when many people are sick.
The town has empty streets and is closed.

The playground, library, and restaurants are closed. Speedy is hungry for French fries. He will look for them at the beach.

Speedy does not find any French fries.

The virus has slowed him down.
He cannot fly super-fast.
Flying super-fast in the sky is his
happy ever after place.

Speedy looks for Timmy.

Speedy asks Timmy for help.
Timmy says, "Let's talk to our unicorn friends.
They are high in the sky."

They tell the unicorns about the pandemic.

The unicorns listen.

The unicorns say, " We have magical unicorn dust to end the pandemic. We will go home to get the magical dust."

Timmy is sad.
He stays busy with his seashell collection.
He hopes the unicorns will return soon.

Timmy is lonely.

There is no one at the beach.

His happy ever after place is a beach with children laughing and playing.

Speedy is an unhappy seagull.
He also misses the children on the beach.
He wants his zoom superpower back.

Speedy is very hungry.
There are no French fries on the beach today.
He hopes the beach will open soon.

Every day, Timmy looks for a rainbow.
The rainbow means the unicorns are near.
They will bring the magical dust to end the
pandemic.

The rain has stopped. The waves are high.
But there is no rainbow today.

One day Timmy sees a rainbow.
The unicorns have returned.
He is happy to see his friends.
He smiles and waves to them.

The unicorns say, "Here is the magical unicorn dust. Sprinkle it everywhere. The pandemic will end tomorrow."

Timmy finds Speedy on the beach.
He says, "I saw our unicorn friends.
They gave me the magical unicorn dust.
Please sprinkle it around.
Tomorrow, the pandemic will end."

Speedy smiles and is happy.
He says, "Yes, I will sprinkle it everywhere.
I will ask my seagull friends to help."

Speedy says to his friends,
"I have the magical unicorn dust.
Let's sprinkle it everywhere today.
Tomorrow the pandemic will be over."

The seagulls shout, "Let's go, seagull team. This magical unicorn dust will end the pandemic. Up, up, and away we go!"

Speedy says, "It is time to nap, Timmy.
I am tired from sprinkling the magical dust.
Tomorrow the pandemic will be over.
Sweet dreams, my friend."

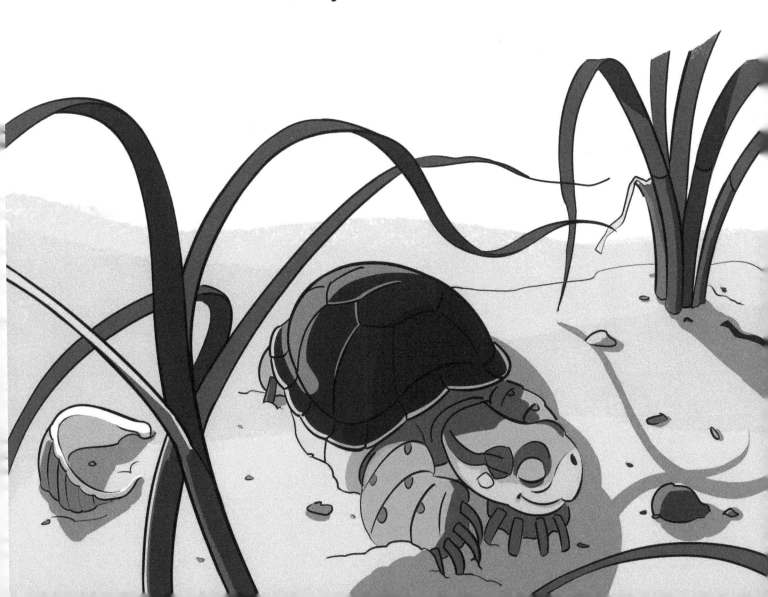

Speedy falls asleep.
He has a happy ever after dream.
He dreams of flying super-fast over a
beach full of French fries.

Magically, the pandemic is over.
The beach and town are open.

Restaurants are serving French fries.

Timmy and Speedy are happy.
Speedy has his zoom superpower back.

Speedy says, "Goodbye. Time to find French fries."

The seagulls are happy.
They fly high and share French fries.

They are happy to be part of the team.
It took teamwork to end the pandemic.

Timmy is tired and happy.
He tries to take a nap.
But he hears noises.

There are children on the beach.
They are playing with their toys.
They are singing happy songs.

They sing, "Hooray.
A happy day to swim and play."

The magical unicorn dust ended the pandemic. Speedy has his zoom superpower back.

Speedy Seagull, Timmy Turtle, and the unicorns are friends forever. They live *happy ever after·*

Happy coloring.

Happy coloring.

Glossary

- disease (noun)
an illness of people,
plants, or animals
caused by an infection

- pandemic (noun)
a disease that exists in
almost all of a group of people,
animals, or plants

- virus (noun)
a very small organism that causes disease in humans,
animals, and plants. A virus is also a disease caused by
a virus.

All definitions from the following source: Cambridge
University Press, (2022),
Cambridge Dictionary, English Dictionary, https://
dictionary.cambridge.org/dictionary/english/

Happy Talking Points

1. What is Speedy Seagull's superpower?
2. What is Speedy Seagull's favorite food?
3. What do the unicorns give to Timmy Turtle to end the pandemic?
4. What does Timmy Turtle collect on the beach?
5. What is your favorite color in the rainbow?
6. Tell us about your happy ever after place.

Answers:
1. Zoom, flying super-fast
2. French fries
3. Magical unicorn dust
4. Seashells
5. My favorite color is...
6. My happy ever after place is...

About the Author

Dr Marlene MD is passionate about creative writing and spoken word. In November 2020, her fictional short story *The Day the Unicorns came to Delray Beach* was the first runner-up in the Delray Beach Library Pen to Pandemic Short Story contest, Delray Beach, Florida. *Happy Ever After A Pandemic Tale* was born.

In April 2021, Her book, Serenity View: Poems and Images of the Blue Ridge Mountains was published. Her articles, chapters, and poems appear in medical textbooks, magazines, and newsletter. She performs spoken word using her poetry.

She has a medical degree (MD) and is a Fellow of the American Academy of Family Physicians. She retired from clinical family medicine in 2015. She presently is an Adjunct Assistant Professor teaching nutrition at the graduate school level.

She is a Distinguished Toastmaster (DTM), fine-tuning her written and spoken word. She enjoys cooking, Mah Jongg, her orchids, and playing with her grandchildren.

Enjoy her written words at www.DrMarleneMD.com

****

HAPPY EVER AFTER PICNIC

for our new neighbor,
Pelican Pat
Join us on the beach for
good food and happy times

Your friends,
The Unicorns
Picnic Date: 2023

****

Our new neighbor is so nice!

CPSIA information can be obtained
at www.ICGtesting.com
Printed in the USA
BVHW021322170722
642290BV00006B/135

9 781088 029282